50¢

D1317836

OTHER PICTURE BOOKS BY
GERALD ROSE

The Bag of Wind
How George Lost His Voice
How St Francis Tamed the Wolf
(with text by Elizabeth Rose)
PB On Ice
PB Takes a Holiday

British Library Cataloguing
in Publication Data
Rose, Gerald, *1935–*
Scruff.
I. Title
823′.914 [J] PZ7
ISBN 0–370–30619–8

Copyright © Gerald Rose 1984
Printed in Great Britain for
The Bodley Head Ltd,
9 Bow Street, London WC2E 7AL
by William Clowes Ltd, Beccles
First published 1984

Scruff

Gerald Rose

THE BODLEY HEAD
London · Sydney · Toronto

Scruff had a very sensitive nose. He could
smell things from a long way off.
 He could smell squirrels up trees . . .

Woof Woof

rabbits in their burrows and old bones that he had
forgotten he had buried deep in the garden.

One day at breakfast Grandad said, ''Poof! What's that odd smell?''

''I can't smell a thing with this cold,'' said Grandma. ''Perhaps it's your egg.''

Scruff decided to find out what the strange smell could be. He sniffed Grandad's dirty socks and his terrible tobacco.

He went into the garden and sniffed
the compost heap...

Sniff
Sniff

and the next-door neighbour's bonfire, but there was nothing odd about any of these smells.

Just then Grandma called Scruff to come shopping with her. As they walked past some wet paint, Scruff growled quietly to himself. He did not like paint smells at all.

Grandma went into the chemist's to buy some cough mixture.

"Pooh! Where did that unpleasant smell come from?" said the chemist.

Scruff sniffed the toothpaste, soap and perfumes. Yes, he thought, there *is* a funny smell around here.

In the next shop the greengrocer
said, "Phew! What's that peculiar smell?"
"It's probably those ripe bananas
of yours!" said Grandma.

Sniff
Sniff

The fishmonger in the market wrinkled his nose and sniffed very loudly.

"There's a nasty smell," he complained.

Scruff also sniffed very loudly.

The fish smelt fine to him.

Sniff
Sniff

At the next stall the cheeseseller said, "I can smell something dreadful!"

"I expect it's your blue cheese," said Grandma. "It's enough to frighten the mice away!"

Finally, Grandma bought some flowers.
"Pooh! What an awful smell! You'll need these roses!" said the florist.

As they walked home, Scruff sniffed lots of strange smells – petrol fumes,

Cough Cough

unemptied dustbins,
mucky shoes,

cosseted cats and an old boot.
   Could one of these be the
smell everyone was complaining
about?

Sniff
Sniff

When they reached home, they found they had two young visitors.

"Poof! That dog STINKS!" cried Tim and Debbie.

"Well I never!" said Grandma. "So that's what the smell was! We'd better give him a bath."

So they filled a tub with water and put
Scruff in it.
    They scrubbed him

and rinsed him,

and dried him

and brushed him . . .

Until all the odd,
peculiar,
unpleasant,
nasty,
awful smells
had quite
disappeared.

At least for a little while . . .